Stories and rhymes in this book

MEET THE SCAREDY CATS

THE SCARY STORM

CATALOGUE

THE MIDNIGHT MOUSE

SOME CATS

DON'T BE SCARED — SMILE!

WHAT'S BIG, GREEN AND WOBBLY?

A SCAREDY CAT HAT

Published by Ladybird Books Ltd
27 Wrights Lane London W8 5TZ
A Penguin Company
© LADYBIRD BOOKS LTD MCMXCIX
Produced for Ladybird Books Ltd by Nicola Baxter and Amanda Hawkes
The moral rights of the author/illustrator have been asserted
LADYBIRD and the device of a Ladybird are trademarks of Ladybird Books Ltd

The
Scaredy
Cats

by Ronne Randall

illustrated by Tania Hurt-Newton

Ladybird

MEET THE SCAREDY CATS!

Here's
Scaredy Lil

and Scaredy
Jill...

And their
daddy,
Scaredy Bill.

Last of all,
is Granny
Small!

They're scared of shadows and scared of noise.

They're even scared of cuddly toys!

And I have heard — can it be true? — The Scaredy Cats are scared of... YOU!

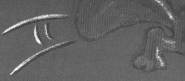

THE SCARY STORM

One morning,
Scaredy Lil
and Scaredy
Jill looked
out of the
window.

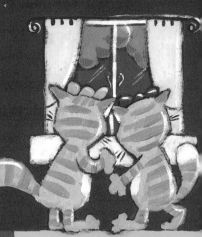

Heavy grey
clouds filled
the sky.

"I'm scared,"
said Scaredy
Jill.

"Don't worry, kittens," said their dad, Scaredy Bill.

"It just means there's rain on the way."

Suddenly, there was a flash of light and a CRASH!

BANG!

BOOM!

"Eeeyikes!" The Scaredy Cats leapt behind the sofa.

Thunder boomed, lightning flashed and rain splattered and splashed.

The three Scaredy Cats huddled together, trembling.

"I'm sooo scaaared," yowled Scaredy Lil.

Then, all at once, everything was quiet.

Slowly,
the three
Scaredy
Cats peeped
out from
behind
the sofa.

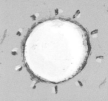

"The sun's
shining!"
said Dad.

"The storm
is over!"
said Lil.

"Oh! Look!"
said Jill...

"There's a beautiful rainbow in the sky!"

"Next time there's a storm," said Scaredy Lil, "I won't be scared."

"Nor will I," said Scaredy Jill, "now that I know what can come after it!"

CATALOGUE

There are
fluffy cats,

And scruffy
cats,

And cats who run around.

But the funniest cats
Are Scaredy Cats,
Who JUMP at every sound!

THE MIDNIGHT MOUSE

Late one night, Scaredy Bill was feeling hungry.

He went to the kitchen to get a snack.

SCRITCH!
SCRATCH!
SCRABBLE!

"Help!" cried
Scaredy Bill.
"Who's
there?"

Suddenly he saw a little tail peeping out from behind the fridge.

"Oh, nooo!" cried Scaredy Bill. "It's a mouse!"

A moment later,
a little face
peeped out.

"Are YOU
scared of
ME?"
squeaked
the mouse.

"Yes, I am!"
said Scaredy Bill.
"Please go away!"

"I don't want to eat you," said Scaredy Bill.

"I want a cheese and cucumber sandwich."

"Ooh, that sounds nice!" said the mouse. "Can I have one?"

So Scaredy Bill made two cheese and cucumber sandwiches...

and a new
friend!

SOME CATS

Some cats go exploring...

Through fields and woods they roam.

Some cats LOVE adventure,

But Scaredy Cats stay...

at home!

DON'T BE SCARED — SMILE!

Scaredy Lil and Scaredy
Jill decided to play a
special scary trick on
Granny Small.

"Let's make some scary masks," said Lil.

all sorts of Scary Masks

"Okay!"
said Jill.
"We can wait until Granny
goes to bed tonight...

then sneak into her room and give her a funny fright!"

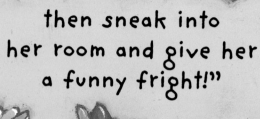

So they drew horrible monster masks...

then hid them away.

When Granny went to bed
that evening, Lil gave Jill
a secret smile.

Then they
put on their
masks...

and
crept up
the stairs.

They tiptoed to Granny's room, ever-so-quietly opened the door and...

"Aaaaagh!"
screamed Jill.

"Waaaagh!"
screamed Lil.

A set of
gleaming
white teeth
grinned at
them in the
moonlight!

The two turned and ran, right into the arms of...

"Granny!" they cried. "Don't go into your room! There's something horrible and SCARY in there!"

"Really?" said Granny, with a toothless smile. "I may be a Scaredy Cat...

but I've never been scared of my own false teeth!"

WHAT'S BIG AND GREEN AND WOBBLY?

One day, Jill's and Lil's cousins, Tabby Tim and Tabby Tom, came for a visit.

Jill and Lil helped to unpack their case.

"WAAAH!
What's that?"
shouted Jill.

"That's only
my cuddly
panda,"
said Tom.

"It scared me!" said Jill.

Later, the four cousins played in the garden.

"OH-OOOH!" cried Lil.

as something fluttered in front of her.

"It's only a
butterfly!"
said Tim.

"But it
scared US!"
said Jill.

Soon Dad
called all
the kittens
in for lunch.

Four hungry kittens sat down eagerly at the table.

Dad came in from the kitchen, carrying a big platter.

There was something big and green and wobbly on the platter.

"YOWWWL!" cried Tim and Tom in terror. "What's THAT?"

Jill and Lil laughed. "That's only Dad's special jelly and catnip ice cream surprise!"

"Well, it SCARED us!" laughed
Tim and Tom.

A SCAREDY CAT HAT

One Scaredy Cat hides behind the door.

Two Scaredy Cats creep along the floor.

Three Scaredy Cats quake
under the rug...

Four
Scaredy
Cats share
a great
big hug!